Let's All be Ambassadors for a Better World

Copyright © 2021 by Denis G. Antoine

All rights reserved. No part of this publication may be reproduced, distributed, or transmitted in any form or by any means, including photocopying, recording, or other electronic or mechanical methods, without the prior written permission of the publisher, except in the case of brief quotations embodied in critical reviews and certain other noncommercial uses permitted by copyright law. For permission requests, write to the author, addressed "Attention: Publisher" at the email address below.

ISBN: 978-1-7358525-5-3

Ordering Information:
Quantity sales. Special discounts are available on quantity purchases by churches, associations, and others. For details, contact the author at the address below. Orders by U.S. trade bookstores and wholesalers. Please email: cpaul@aknowingspirit.com.

Publisher Mailing Address:
Aknowingspirit, LLC
P.O. Box 3324
Washington, D.C. 20010

Dedicated to all,
and future ambassadors.

One Friday afternoon while Dun and Gre played in a park. Dun had an idea that came like a little spark.

"Hey Gre, what's an ambassador? What do they do?"

Gre shrugged his shoulders, "Hmm…You have lots of questions, but I don't have a clue."

The kids were stumped, but then another thought came their way.

"Well, let us ask our principal on Monday to hear what she has to say."

At 9:00 a.m. on Monday morning, Dun and Gre arrived at school. They marched right up to the principal's office to learn what ambassadors do.

"Good morning, Madam Principal, before we go to class, we have important questions that we can't wait to ask."

"Okay," the principal responded, sitting up at attention with poise. She even turned down her radio to cut out all the noise.

"Please ask, you have my interest, come on, I insist."

Dun looked at Gre and said, "Ok, we made a list."

"We would like to know what's an ambassador, what do ambassadors do, and where do they go?"

"Hmmm...those are interesting questions." The Principal said, "I'd also like to know."

"I am pleased that you have interest in this profession of which I have a lot to learn. Thursday is career day at our school, how about we give an ambassador a turn?"

"Great suggestion, madam principal," Dun responded. Gre soon chimed in with a suggested guest, "My neighbor is an ambassador and he is the very best!"

"That is a great proposal," the principal agreed. "But we must let your neighbor know, and confirm his availability. I will prepare an invitation for our mystery man. But can I count on you to deliver this letter with care by hand?"

The kids responded, "Of course, madam principal! You can surely count on us."

There was no time for playing today, they had to catch the bus.

As soon as the bus stopped, Dun and Gre hurried to the neighbor's door. Knock, knock. They both were impatient and decided to knock once more.

The door opened slowly, "Good afternoon, Mr. Denis! We have something for you to see."

They handed Mr. Denis the letter, "Oh, thank you. I wonder what it could be?"

He opened the letter with a bit of cheer, "Could you please join us on Thursday to tell us about your career?"

After reading those words, Mr. Denis said, "I happily accept!" with a pleased grin. "Thursday, is a busy morning, but I'll arrive on time at ten!"

Early Thursday morning, on Career Day, Dun and Gre arrived beaming with pride. They spread the word that a mystery guest is coming and more children rushed inside.

The students lined up and walked, well-behaved to the assembly hall. So much excitement filled the room, they did not wait for teachers to call.

Gre and Dun couldn't contain themselves because they were the only ones that knew the secret guest. But soon, and very soon, so would all the rest.

The principal entered the assembly hall, "Good morning teachers, students. Greetings to all."

With wide eyes she looked around, "Are you ready to have fun? Today, we have a surprise visitor, who was invited by Gre and Dun."

"Welcome to Career Day, our program is about to begin. And look we are right on time, the clock just struck ten."

The Principal instructed, "Gre and Dun, please escort our invitee to the front of the room. Children please settle down, the program will start soon."

The visitor was escorted to the podium, there he stood, smiled, and looked around.

"Thank you for having me." Then he gently placed his briefcase on the ground.

The Principal looked at the visitor and said, "Welcome again, we have a huge task for you. The students have many questions about what ambassadors do."

"Our students are very interested in your career, once again we can't thank you enough for being here."

Our first question is from Dun and Gre. They asked, can you please tell us what is an ambassador?

"Madam Principal, teachers, and children, thank you for your invitation. And thank you Gre and Dun for proposing that I come; and for your great question."

The Honored guest responded. "I am Mr. Denis, and I am an ambassador, I am no mystery man. Today, I am glad to share, that the word "ambassador" is a title, given to a person who is appointed and sent, by one country to another, to publicly represent. Ambassadors with full powers to conduct business are called Extra-ordinary and Pleni-poten-tiary. An ambassador works from an embassy, with a delegation; with titles such as envoy, attaché, and diplomat. Churches also appoint ambassadors called legates - like the (papal) nuncio. There are chargé de affairs, and deputy ambassadors, that are sent, to serve their country, where ever they go."

"Mr. Ambassador, can you please tell us what you do daily, and where do you go?" Mary expressed.

"By your question I have learned of your interest in my career," the ambassador spoke. "Now I am eager to share, knowing that soon one of you will be standing here." And with a smile, the honored guest carried on. I am glad to tell you that being an ambassador is like being an assayer.

An ambassador's day is full of appointments with serious responsibilities. The day is spent in search of truth, working to build and strengthen good relationships, between countries and among citizens. There is frequent travel to negotiate and reach agreements. Daily, ambassadors seek to find peace, offering and applying solutions to prevent conflicts and wars. Ambassadors work with honor and confidence to convey points of view, positions, and priorities of the government and people they represent. The day-to-day concern of an ambassador is about how to make our world better.

"What are qualities of a good/successful ambassador?" Liam asked, shyly.

A good ambassador must be courteous and strong because they are spokespersons and factual messengers. Ambassadors must be problem solvers and smart in many ways. Effective ambassadors must ensure that their country's interest is well represented every day.

Ambassadors must be full of wit, and ready to speak when called to their feet. A successful ambassador is always well prepared to find and promote truth and cooperation. An envoy must be credible, with knowledge of how to get along, with different cultures, and able to resolve confusion among opponents and friends. Excellent and successful ambassadors must be competent at making sense of global events that flood electronic, print, and broadcast media. Ambassadors must be good advisers to the country they represent. A good ambassador always places first the agenda from the country he was sent.

"What's the fun part of being an ambassador?" Iva asked, with a raised hand.

Ambassadors are protected while they serve, by an agreement called the Vienna Convention, which provides safety, while working within the receiving country. Privileges and exemptions are provided to help an ambassador work with ease, and to foster welcoming relations by the receiving nation. Meeting people, learning to understand them and their culture, makes it most enjoyable being an ambassador. Also, always being treated as a guest is special. Messages to and from an ambassador's homeland are given privacy. There is a feeling that an ambassador's work is important because the embassies, residencies and properties of ambassadors are regarded as sovereign space. There is freedom to work without obstruction. It is important and enjoyable to attend special events - such as national day celebrations of the host and other countries. A very special occasion for an ambassador is an invitation to a school, to meet teachers and speak to children. Ambassadors get to visit many new places to explore and share about their country, their culture, and other priorities. There are many learning experiences, which bring excitement and enlightenment. "It is fun to achieve the objectives for which you were sent," the ambassador elaborated.

"How can I become an ambassador?" Gemma called out.

Great question, Gemma. Becoming an ambassador can begin right here at school. It is important to know what kind of ambassador you want to be. To be an ambassador requires a lot of preparation. It begins with the practice of humility, being knowledgeable, honorable, and well-informed. Ambassadors may be sent to a country to work between that country and his country (bi-lateral). Ambassadors are sent to the United Nations, and the Organization of American States (OAS); to other regional and global, bodies, to conduct many-sided negotiations. Working between many countries (multi-lateral). Persons are chosen carefully, for their knowledge, skills, and professional training, to function as ambassadors for different causes. The United Nations Secretary-General appoints couriers, to promote world peace and harmony. They are called Goodwill Ambassadors. There are outstanding performers and promoters named ambassadors for special activities like the arts, culture, and industries". Mr. Denis encouraged the students by saying, "Begin by becoming the head of your class. Lead the field in your subject of choice and become the best. Just remember that it takes real sacrifice. Begin by standing as an ambassador for your family, by always keeping your conduct excellent.

Wherever you are sent you are a representative of your home. Students in the assembly hall nodded with understanding. "There are ambassadors that speak up for the environment, religion, and the rights of children.

They are envoys for better understanding among human beings," Mr. Denis spelled out. Some students murmured but continued looking on with fascination. Seeing the students' attention, Mr. Denis continued, "Plan to become a world leader then you are a head ambassador. Be the secretary-general of the United Nations. Become a pope or a rabbi, imam, or pastor or any other; make your choice. But remember, there is always room for citizen ambassadors with good character, strong social standings and excellent reputations."

With excitement Iva shouted, "Can I be an ambassador?"

"Certainly!" the ambassador replied. "We can all be ambassadors in our respective positions. As you can now tell an ambassador is more than a title, it is character, conduct and effective personality."
Parents are ambassadors, of their families; school principals are ambassadors of their schools. Doctors and teachers are cool health and education ambassadors. And your classmates who are prefects are classroom envoys. There are ambassadors in all fields of study, science, math, and technology. I know some leading political ambassadors like Prime Minister Keith Mitchell of Grenada, and President Joe Biden of the USA. Amanda Gorman of the USA and Ricardo Keens-Douglas of Grenada are poets and literary ambassadors.
Olympians like Kirani James of Grenada and Usain Bolt of Jamaica are ambassadors because they are sports stars. So, when one represents a country whether it's United States, Canada, China, Malaysia, or Grenada; in whatever capacity with dignity, you are an emissary.

Whichever career you choose, when you excel, you are an ambassador as well. Ambassadors work to promote unity, compassion, and equality. They are capable and do not work for fame. There are ambassadors that represent, just to promote kindness in every field. Now you can represent your class, your group, or your friend, by becoming an expert for the good you choose. "When anyone asks you what your name is? Represent yourself; answer with certainty, please. Get ready to take your place as health and science ambassadors, represent wellness and find cures. We all need to be ambassadors, for the poor, the deprived, those that cannot speak, our animals, for the strong and weak. When every human being is an ambassador, we can represent one and other. There will be speedy reconciliation, no need to fight for justice. Disputes would be resolved without hostility, with more listening, there would be less hurting, and we would all be involved in achieving the best for the totality of humanity, because that's what ambassadors do." Mr. Denis disclosed. Our world needs more ambassadors, in the work to find cures for deadly disease, destroy ill-wills, and resolve all prejudices and differences. Become an ambassador and lets free up our world, please."

Dun stood up and calmly said to Gre, "I want to be an ambassador, so I can represent; our world is ready, and I am ready, are you?"

Gre burst out, "Thank you, Mr. Ambassador!" This is a great career and today I know what I want to be."

Gre stood up and shouted to the assembly, "LETS ALL BE AMBASSADORS FOR A BETTER WORLD!"

About the Author

 H.E. Denis G. Antoine, PhD has more than twenty (20) years of high-level bilateral and diplomatic experience in North America, Latin America, and the multilateral systems of the United Nations, and the Organization of American States, in the Inter-American System, and globally.

Ambassador Antoine served as Ambassador Extraordinary and Plenipotentiary of Grenada to the People's Republic of China (PRC) from 2016 to 2019. Denis G. Antoine has also served as Ambassador / Permanent Representative to the United Nations, where he served as Vice President to the 69th Session of the United Nations General Assembly from 2013 to 2016. Before serving at the United Nations, he was Ambassador At-Large and Director of the Office of International Programs and Exchange at the University of the District of Columbia in Washington, D.C. from 2009 to 2013.

H.E. Denis G. Antoine also had an unprecedented tour of duty as Grenada's Ambassador to the United States of America and Permanent Representative to the Organization of American States (OAS) in Washington, D.C. and concurrently, he was non-resident Ambassador to Mexico and Panama, from 1995 to 2009. When he demitted Office in 2009, he was the second highest ranking ambassador to the United States in Washington D.C.

CPSIA information can be obtained
at www.ICGtesting.com
Printed in the USA
BVHW022049010921
615375BV00002B/27